As it wasn't to be with Asun, for Asun.

I.M.

Could it happen to anyone?

Text © 2011 Mar Pavon
Illustrations © 2011 Sonja Wimmer
This edition © 2011 Cuento de Luz SL
Calle Claveles 10 | Urb Monteclaro | Pozuelo de Alarcón | 28223 Madrid | Spain | www.cuentodeluz.com
Original title in Spanish: ¿Puede pasarle a cualquiera?
English translation by Jon Brokenbrow

ISBN: 978-84-152410-3-4

Printed by Shanghai Chenxi Printing Co Ltd in PRC, April 2011, print number 1186-01

FSC
www.fsc.org
MIX
Paper from
responsible sources
FSC® C007923

CUENTO
DE LUZ

Mar Pavon

Sonja Wimmer

COULD it
happen to
anyone?

Today, after leaving school,
Balzo goes shopping with his Mom.
They go into one of those stores
where children can't touch anything.
Time drags on, and Balzo is
bored stiff. And there isn't even
a chair to sit down on!
But Mom is having a great time,
touching and feeling all the pretty things.

It's not fair! thinks Balzo.

And as he can't stand it any more,

he sits down on the floor and pretends he's a silkworm.

Balzo the silkworm decides to explore the store

DONOTTOUCH in search of adventures. Of course,

he does it by wriggling across the floor.

Otherwise, the game wouldn't be any fun!

Balzo wriggles towards the counter.

But, when he arrives, he realizes that a counter

doesn't really have anything interesting to offer

an adventurous silkworm like him.

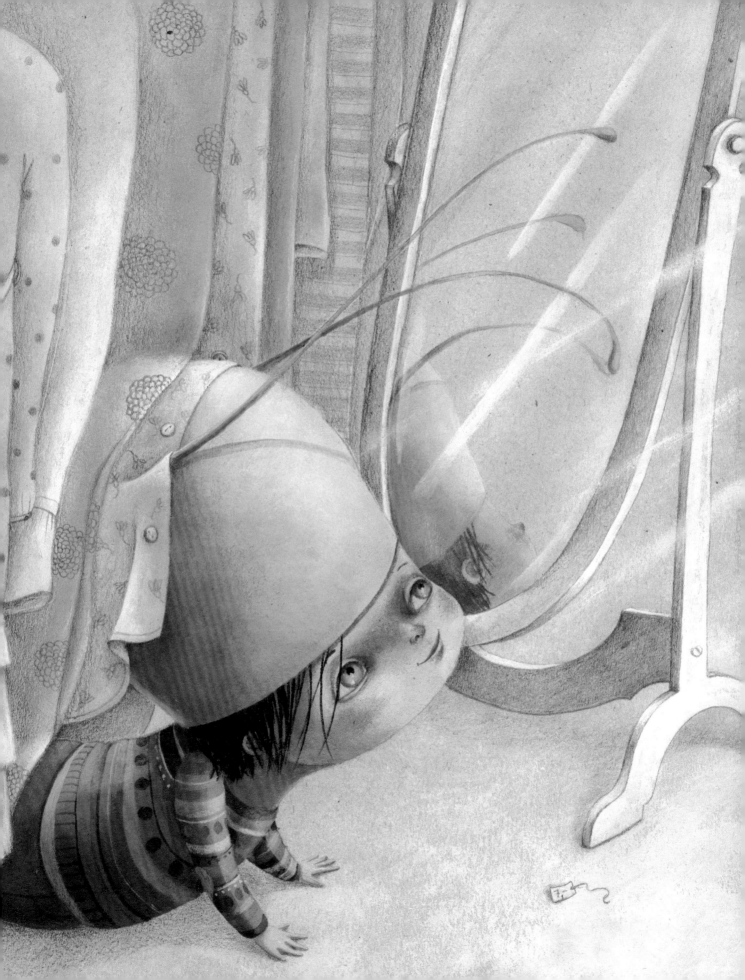

Now, Balzo wriggles towards
a shelf full of beautiful figurines.
When he gets there, his eyes
open wide in wonder.

There's a monkey eating a coconut.
A mermaid with a bow tied to her tail.
Three clowns dancing in a circle.
A boy and a girl kissing each other.
A butterfly sitting on top
of a bald man's head…

That's it! The silkworm decides it's time
to turn into a butterfly.
Isn't that what all of the
silkworms do?
Although, of course, to be a butterfly,
first you have to cuddle up under the shelves,
where nobody can see you...
and wrap yourself up in a cocoon!

But Balzo can't be wrapped up for too long,
because Mom suddenly starts to call out:
"Balzo, honey, where are you hiding?"
Then Balzo decides to surprise Mom:
He'll flutter over to her through the air!
Isn't that what all butterflies do?

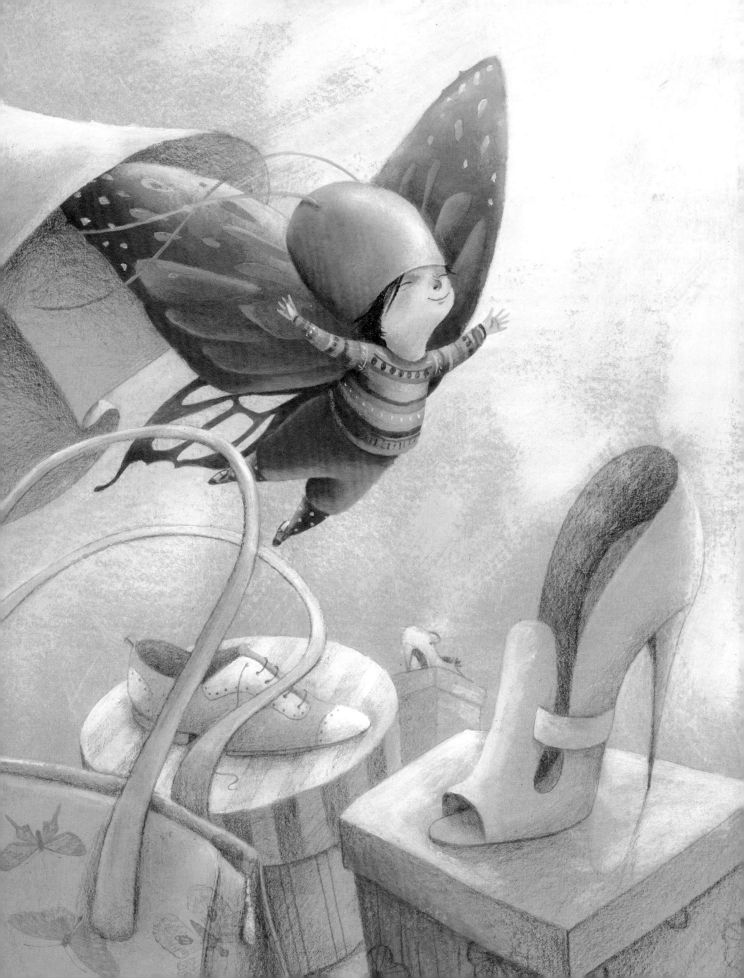

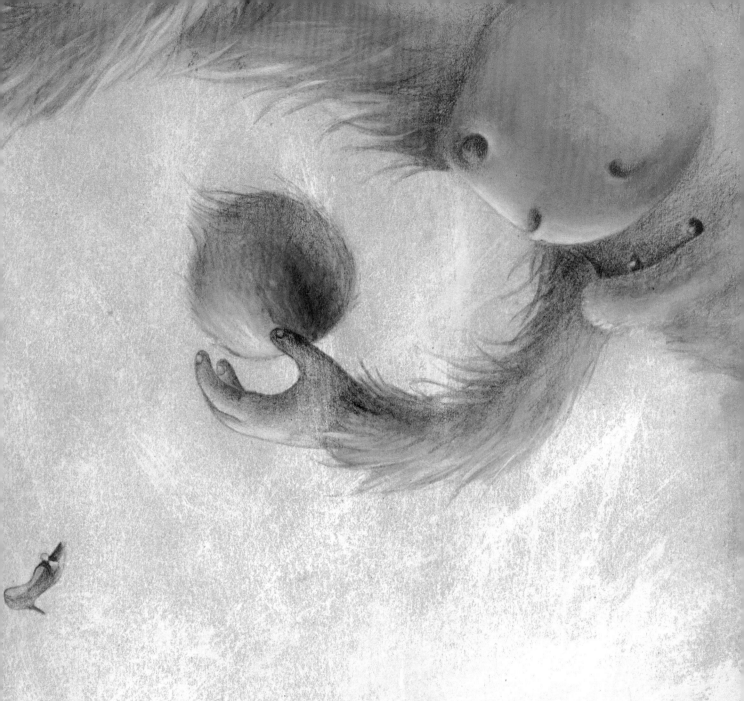

Oh no! When he tries to get on his knees to break out of the cocoon
and fly towards Mom, he forgets there are shelves above him…
CLUNK! He hits them with his head, and instead it's the figurines that go flying…
and CRASH! They all come tumbling down noisily onto the floor.

Balzo, a little dazed from knocking his head,
looks around him and…oh, what a mess!
The monkey has lost his coconut!
The mermaid has lost her bow!
The clowns aren't holding hands!
The boy and girl aren't kissing!
The butterfly has lost its bald spot!
Balzo is the only one who's got something:
a big lump on his head!

Mom and the storekeeper run over,
And when they see what's happened, they look like ogres.
The storekeeper puts his hands on his head
as if he had a lump there too, and growls:
"Well ma'am, you're going to have to pay for all this damage!
And you're going to have to teach your son not to touch things!"

Mom blushes with embarrassment, and says "Yes, yes"
lots of times, and between saying "Yes, yes", she threatens
Balzo with the worst thing you can say to a child
who's broken something by accident:
"WE'LL TALK ABOUT THIS AT HOME!"
And all the while, nobody's worried about the lump,
maybe because it's still a newly-hatched lump.

When they get home, Mom, whose voice
still sounds like an ogre's, tells off Balzo for
touching everything. And when he tells her
he didn't touch anything, she tells him off
for telling a lie. And when Balzo tells her
that he's really, really, really telling the truth,
she says he's got his head in the clouds!
She only starts to believe him a little because
of the lump, because like any lump worth
mentioning, it keeps growing and growing
on his head.

After he has his dinner, Balzo is so tired and has such a headache,
that he goes straight to bed. Mom, who's stopped being an ogre by now,
gives him a goodnight kiss on his forehead, but she forgets to kiss
his lump, which by now is the size of an egg.
Later on, Dad comes into Balzo's room and gives him a big hug,
but darn it! He forgets to kiss his lump too, which by now
has gotten so big, it's been named the King of Lumps.

Balzo is just about to close his eyes, when
suddenly there's a loud CRASH, very similar to
the one he caused in the DONOTTOUCH store.
Then he hears Mom's voice:
"Oh no! I've smashed the Chinese vase!
It just slipped out of my hands!"
To which Dad says:
"Well, never mind. It could happen to anyone!"
And his voice doesn't sound like an ogre's;
instead, quite the opposite: it's so calm...!

Balzo, laying in his bed, doesn't understand.
What does he mean "it could happen to anyone"?
Why did they get so angry with him this afternoon?
And he didn't even touch the figurines!
But all the same, Balzo finally falls asleep.
And can you guess what he dreams about?

He dreams that the monkey without his coconut, the mermaid without her bow, the clowns without their circle, the couple without the kiss, and the butterfly without the bald spot all come to visit him at home.

But instead of telling him off,
the monkey grunts:
"Never mind how delicious the coconut was,
it could happen to anyone!"

And the mermaid sings to him:
"Never mind how pretty the bow was,
it could happen to anyone!"

And the clowns all yell:
"Never mind how much fun it was to dance in a circle,
it could happen to anyone!"

The boy and the girl say:
"Never mind how sweet the kiss was,
it could happen to anyone!"

And the butterfly whispers:
"Never mind how smooth the bald patch was,
it could happen to anyone!"

Because this, believe me, is the best thing that you can say to anyone (it doesn't matter if it's a child or a grown-up) who's just broken something by accident.
And then, straight away, they head towards the refrigerator to find some ice cubes…

And they take care of the really important thing
in all of this tale: GETTING RID OF HIS HORRIBLE
(AND HUUUUGE) LUMP!